P9-DME-396

For Boo
E.G.

First published in North America in 2017 by Boxer Books Limited.
www.boxerbooks.com
Boxer® is a registered trademark of Boxer Books Limited.
Text and illustrations copyright © 2017 Emma Garcia
The right of Emma Garcia to be identified as the author and illustrator
of this work has been asserted by her in accordance with the Copyright, Designs and Patents Act, 1988.
All rights reserved, including the right of reproduction in whole or in part in any form.
Library of Congress Cataloging-in-Publication Data available.
The illustrations were prepared using hand-printed paper and acrylic paints.
The text is set in American Typewriter.

ISBN 978-1-910716-23-6
1 3 5 7 9 10 8 6 4 2

Printed in China

All of our papers are sourced from managed forests and renewable resources.

Chugga Chugga Choo Choo

Emma Garcia

Boxer Books

Chugga Chugga

4 3 2

... here comes the train!

Choo Choo

Clickety clack on the track.
Going to . . .

4 3 2 1

. . . the
seaside.

We can
taste the
ice cream.

here comes the train!

Clickety clack
on the track.
Going to . . .

. . . the **forest**.

We can hear
the **birds sing**.

Chugga Chugga Choo Choo

here comes the train!

Clickety clack on the track.
Going to . . .

. . . the **city**.

We can see the **tall buildings**.

Clickety clack on the track.
Going to . . .

. . . the **farm**.

We can smell the **farmyard**!

2 1

Chugga Chugga Choo Choo

here comes the train!

. . . **the station** for a nice long rest.

But who is making all that noise?

Shoo, shoo!

Fly away, birds.

Night, night, train.

See you tomorrow.